Cosy Burrow Books

VALKYRIE ACADEMY DRAGON ALLIANCE
Book Eight

ABDUCTED

I0594622

"*Abducted* is wonderfully infused with Norse mythology, including angels of death, Valkyries, and of course, Loki at his finest." Amanda K., Line Editor, Red Adept Editing

Valkyrie Academy Dragon Alliance Books

Marked (Prequel)
Chosen
Vanished
Scorned
Inflicted
Empowered
Ambushed
Warned
Abducted
Besieged
Deceived

Cosy Burrow Books

VALKYRIE ACADEMY DRAGON ALLIANCE

ABDUCTED

KATRINA COPE

Michael ~ your support means the world to me

Through this link you can sign up for my newsletter and receive a FREE copy of Marked plus updates about my fantasy books, sales and notification of giveaways.

- CHAPTER ONE -

My body jerks sideways, and my legs fling wildly in the opposite direction before colliding with the giant's stomach. The thump reverberates through my body and into my brain. A throbbing headache grows with each passing moment as I'm flung around some more.

The giant has me firmly in his grasp facing outward, and no matter how hard I try, I cannot free myself. I kick his stomach, bite his enormous fingers, jam my knees against his arm and hand, I even pull any of his hair I can grasp between my teeth, but his clasp doesn't waver. The only beings who will know that I'm missing are the guards that the giant rendered unconscious once they wake. Elan was too far away when I was taken from Asgard to call to for help. No one will come looking for me, which leaves escape as my only option, but I can't fight anymore. My arms ache from the effort to free them from his grasp, and the pressure he's applying to my waist is making my body throb. Exhausted, I quit fighting and wait for his next move until I see our intended destination.

After climbing down for a while, the giant pauses in the branches of Yggdrasil, the world tree, and his blue hand releases the pressure of his grip around me. I use the opportunity to kick and fight some more, calling on every morsel of strength I have left, but to no avail.

He still has ahold of me, but his grip is loose enough that I can wriggle my arms out of his grasp. Finally, having my hands free, I pull on my magic, willing it to gather inside of me until he pulls out a rope and ties my hands securely by my sides with my palms pinned to my thighs. He grabs me by the back of my leather top, roughly shoves my long hair aside, and raises me toward his face. Hot breath steams the back of my neck as I kick and thrash, trying to strike him. This can't be my end. Surely my fate is not to be eaten by a giant. In my moment of panic, my arms and body turn numb.

I'm yanked backward, and roughly, the back of my top is shoved between something hard. Something wet drips onto the skin of my shoulder. The intensity of the hot breath increases, and I screw up my nose as I smell rotten flesh on his breath. I can do nothing to save myself. I scrunch my eyes closed. I don't want to watch while he eats me.

The next moment, my body swings wildly, and my thighs slam into something hard. I grunt with pain. That's definitely going to leave a bruise. Gathering my courage, I pry one eye open and realize that I slammed into the trunk of Yggdrasil, and my whole body is still swinging. The giant has resumed his climb down the world tree.

Something wet drips down the back of my shirt, and I curl my lip. It feels disgusting. I pry open my other eye and gaze over my shoulder. Now I understand. The collar of my top is wedged between the giant's large brown teeth. He isn't going to eat me, not yet anyway. He must need both hands to climb down the rest of the tree.

"Where are you taking me?" I glance over my shoulder into his eyes and catch the glare he gives me. "What are you glaring at me for? I'm the one who's been taken against my will. I can't help it if I'm curious."

He doesn't answer, which annoys me, but at the same time, I'm relieved. I'm not sure he would remember to take me out of his mouth before speaking. I glance down the trunk of Yggdrasil. That is a long way to fall.

The giant swings down a few more branches then lands on a large, sturdy branch similar to the one he used to exit Asgard. With me still swinging from his mouth, he balances on the branch with his arms spread wide and walks toward the tip. The branch juts through a hole, and on the other side, a strong, chilly wind blows against my skin. My skin instantly grows goose bumps. The air is fresh, a welcome smell after the stench of the giant's breath.

A broad display of snow-tipped mountains greets me, and miles of frozen lakes spread vastly across the land. I haven't been here before, although I gather that this is Jotunheim, the land of the giants.

The giant grabs me roughly in his hand and wraps his arm around me, securing my back against his chest. He bends his knees and jumps off the branch onto the frozen ground. He lands with a thump, and the impact jars me. I shiver. My clothes are still damp from the thunderstorm that passed through Asgard just before I was kidnapped. The giant jogs with large thumping steps, jolting my body with each impact. My head throbs, and I long to be released.

A movement catches my eye, and I gaze at the sky. I'm surprised to see the belly of a yellow dragon flying over us. It circles once, and I spot an animal trapped between its teeth. I shudder. I hope that's not why the giant brought me here. Becoming a dragon's meal is not on my bucket list. Suddenly the dragon dives toward a mountain and disappears.

The frost giant aims toward the same mountain, his head turning in all different directions, as if looking for someone. My heart beats harder as his footsteps never falter. Becoming a dragon lunch is looking more probable for me. I breathe as deeply as I can under the giant's embrace. I need to push aside all worry and focus. It may be my only chance for escape.

As we near the mountain, I spot a large opening in the surface, and he barges through it. I welcome the break from the icy winds. Rocks clatter across the ground with his footsteps, and the sound echoes off the stone walls of the tunnel.

Warmth hits my face, confusing me. It feels as though the tunnel is being warmed with a heat as intense as a fire. I didn't think frost giants needed warmth, although my body doesn't argue. The giant continues to carry me deep inside the mountain until, eventually, we come across a cave off to the side of the tunnel. The frost giant grabs me firmly in both hands, shoves me into the room, then drags the bars across the entrance of the cave, securing them to the side and trapping me within the room.

"What are you going to do with me?" I shuffle toward the bars, ignoring the ache in my leg, which had clipped a large rock while I was being dragged through the tunnel.

"Stay." The giant shakes a finger at me, his voice deep and menacing.

"Why?" I glare at him, clenching my fists by my sides. My magic roars inside me, and I long to use it.

"I am a friend of Gilroma's."

"What?" My voice is high-pitched. "If that's the case, then why did you kidnap me?"

"It's for your own good."

"Really?" I frown and plunk my backside on a nearby rock.

"Odin's guards were taking you back to your academy to see your mistress."

"Yeah. That's what they were told to do. I see my mistress regularly. She is rarely pleased with me."

"She was going to give you a harsh punishment."

"Like that's a shock!" I huff.

"No. You don't understand. It was going to be worse than normal." The giant frowns at me.

"Then I would have dealt with it like I usually do. Are you trying to tell me that being kidnapped by a frost giant is better than whatever punishment Mistress Sigrun was going to dish up for me?"

"Yes." The giant's voice holds finality. I'm about to argue some more when he abruptly turns around and calls over his shoulder, "Stay here," before he walks off.

"Like I have a choice," I call after the giant. Although I probably could break myself out of here with my magic. I wriggle my fingers and thrash my arms. Without the giant securing them, I have a little leeway within the rope. I shuffle my arms, eventually managing to work my hands behind me. Searching for the knot, I stretch my fingers up, just managing to stroke them across a knot resting higher than my grasp. I curse then look around the room. My heartbeat quickens when I spot a sharp edge to the rock I had sat on. I maneuver toward it, stretch a section of rope taut between my thumbs, and set to work rubbing the rope against the rock's sharp surface. After rubbing small patches of skin off, I am rewarded with the sudden release of pressure as the rope snaps.

I glance around the cave, and my excitement is washed away by a spout of annoyance. I'm stuck in some random cage inside a mountain. As if I'm going to listen to the giant who kidnapped me and not use my magic to escape. Besides, it's perfect practice. I also don't know this giant, and he may not be a friend of Gilroma's. He could be bringing someone who will do me harm, or perhaps he is saving me so he can eat me later when he's hungry. So, no. I won't wait here behind bars.

I draw on the magic burning inside me. It's tired of welling and not being released. It wants to be free, and I want to set it free. I aim my hands at the entry point of the bars and blast away the rocks securing them. Shards hit my face as they explode away from the large wall. My face stings where the stones hit me. I touch the aching points, pulling my fingers away when I feel moisture. Blood smears my fingers. The sharp fragments must have lightly sliced my skin. I wipe my cheek on my shoulder, removing some of the excess blood. The cut will heal soon enough with my Valkyrie healing powers.

I focus on another secured spot of bars and blast away the rock, this time raising my arm to protect my face. The point of a flying rock digs into my skin of my arm, and I pull it out, releasing a small stream of blood. I aim my hands at another secured spot, blasting away the rock and repeating the process until the bars wobble free.

My feet crunch on the shards of rock that cover the ground, and I grab the bars and jerk, using the strength of my legs and core. The bars pull away just enough for me to edge through the small gap. As I stand outside my cell, I glance down the stone corridor. I can feel the warmth coming from the center of the mountain. I know that down here, I am sheltered from the breeze, but the air seems warmer than would come from merely removing the icy wind. I stand at the crossroads. I'm tempted to go farther down the tunnel to see why it's so warm, yet at the same time, the pull is strong to leave the way I came. Even though the giant said he was a friend of Gilroma's, that doesn't mean he is. I could be in danger and should escape Jotunheim as soon as possible.

- CHAPTER TWO -

I tiptoe down the corridor from where I came, checking every shadow as I walk past. I want to be sure that nothing will jump out at me. As I progress, I push my back against the side of the wall, and I cautiously approach the entrance with silent feet as my leather shoes hit the ground softly. From behind me, a bright light bursts through the tunnel for a moment, accompanied by a strong gust of heat. It's almost as though a furnace burns in the center of the mountain, ready to combust. If that's so, then it's dangerous to stay down here any longer. If a furnace combusts in the center of a mountain, I can only imagine that it would bring the mountain down with it. I turn around, and the bright light briefly illuminates the full distance of the corridor then dies down. My curiosity is piqued. Despite my thoughts of danger, I debate whether to go back and peek around the corner. I pause in the darkness of the tunnel, staring back to where the light had come from.

"They told me you're a disobedient one," someone says behind me. "I'm impressed. You didn't fail to disappoint."

I spin around to look at the man speaking. My jaw drops when I come face-to-face with the pale skin and sleek form of Loki. His brown eyes narrow over his pointy nose, and his hair is greased back over his shoulder. His black cape blends in perfectly with the dark walls of the tunnel. It takes a few moments for the reality to sink in. My mind whirls with scenarios of why he is here, making it hard to concentrate. I somehow manage to gather my thoughts and close my mouth.

"Loki?"

"In the flesh." Mischief dances in his eyes.

"What are you doing here?" I ask.

He rocks onto his toes then slowly rolls flat onto his feet. "Saving you from another perilous demise."

"But that's going against Odin's orders. You will be in so much trouble if Odin finds out that you intervened with his punishment."

"My dear, have you not heard of my reputation?"

"That you're a mischief-maker and always causing trouble?" I say.

He rolls his hands a few times in a motion to prompt me to go on. When I don't, he continues for me. "And that I never obey Odin's orders, or rarely. I must admit, there was this one time." He studies his fingernails. "But I would be happy if we forgot about that one. I usually obey his orders only when I'm trying to get myself out of trouble."

"But why are you here? Did you bring me here?"

"The land of the giants is my birthplace. It holds a special place in my heart. What you were about to face was another horrible punishment, and you said you wanted to speak with me. So I had one of my ice giant friends kidnap you."

"That was a rather brash kidnapping. That poor frost giant put his life in danger to do that for you."

"Let's just say that he owed me a favor or, rather, his life." Loki chuckles.

I frown. I don't understand the joke.

Loki takes one look at my face and stops chuckling. "Oh, never mind." He waves a hand at me. An inside joke. "So, what did you want to speak with me about?"

I look around the tiny tunnel pressing in on us. I feel trapped and uncomfortable, and being here with the god of mischief, I'm not sure what to think.

Seeing my eyes dart around the tunnel, Loki says, "Why don't we go somewhere more comfortable and a bit more off the track? You know, like the cave you were in only a few moments ago. That's why I asked the giant to leave you there."

I screw up my nose. "Um. It's a little bit damaged."

"We can still stand or sit in there, can't we?"

"If you don't mind standing around crumpled walls and rocks. The cave seems quite safe."

"Or we could go outside and get some fresh air, but I gather it might be too cold for you."

"You gathered right. It's freezing out there. From what I've seen, half the land is frozen, if not more. I think the cave would be better."

"It's not that bad, but let's go back to the cave." He lifts an eyebrow. "I'm keen to see the disarray you left it in."

We walk down the tunnel toward the cave, and when he sees the damage I did, he chuckles. "I see you have lived up to your reputation. You are just as cunning as I've heard."

It suddenly dawns on me. "Hang on. The giant said that Gilroma is one of his friends. And you said the giant is one of your friends. Does that mean that Gilroma is also one of your friends?"

Loki shrugs. "That's one way of putting it."

I grunt. "Can't you ever answer a question properly? You answer everything I ask with a sly comment."

Loki feigns hurt. "That's a bit harsh. I didn't dodge your question. I stated the truth."

I cross my arms over my chest and cock my hip. "Really?"

One side of Loki's mouth lifts in a half smile. "I guess you can call us friends of sorts."

I frown at him. "I know your reputation as a trickster, that you deceive the dragons and gods alike. You're just playing with words when I ask you questions."

"I don't know what you mean."

I let out an exasperated sigh. "Is it going to be like this for our entire conversation?"

Before he answers, a tremendous roar echoes down the tunnel and into the little cave.

- CHAPTER THREE -

I stare down the corridor from the little cave.

"Are there dragons down there?"

Loki's face is straight and lacking emotion when I turn to look at him. If he hadn't known about the dragons farther down the tunnel, he should've been scared, but he isn't.

When he doesn't respond, I interrogate him from a different angle. "Are they dragons from Asgard's wastelands?" When he continues to look emotionless, I try again, determined to find the answer. "Are they from the dragon eggs you stole?"

Loki's jaw drops, and he looks hurt. "Who said I stole dragon eggs?"

I place my hands on my hips and stare at him under a cocked eyebrow. "Are you kidding me? I know you're the zmey."

"What do you mean? Do you really think I'm that hideous creature that flies around Asgard?"

"That's what I've been told."

"By whom?"

I study his expression. I'm surprised at how good he is at deceiving. If I hadn't seen proof, it would be hard not to believe him. "I found a record of some of your shapes in a library book. It states that one of your forms is the zmey. It also says you're the old woman who touched me and the strange young Valkyrie who sat at my dining table one night, looking at the book. The book had precisely those images in it. When I found the book in the library, I was shocked to discover it was titled *Known Shapes of the Shapeshifter Loki.*"

His laugh is high-pitched. "You can't be serious."

My eyes narrow.

He maintains his portrayal of innocence. "Are you telling me you believe in fairy tales out of a storybook?"

Another roar resonates down the tunnel.

"If you're not going to tell me, then I'll just have to have a look." I head out of the cave and down the corridor toward the roar, hoping that the dragons are tame and won't attack. Holding my brave gait, I call over my shoulder, "If I'm not mistaken, that's a dragon roar. I saw a yellow dragon flying above when I was being carried here by the frost giant."

Loki holds out his hand as though to stop me and jogs after me. "I wouldn't go down there if I were you."

"And why not?"

"The dragon will probably eat you." Loki sounds panicked.

"Don't you think I can handle a dragon? I've handled many dragons recently, even aggressive ones." I continue to trek down the tunnel, listening to Loki's hurried footsteps on the stone floor as he struggles to catch up to me. He stumbles, and I smile to myself. He's either worried about my safety or about me discovering his secret. Either way, I'm going to find out.

It doesn't take long to reach the end of the tunnel. As I near the corner, a bright light blasts, illuminating the immediate corridor. Another roar follows, and slowly I edge my head around the corner. My jaw drops, and I retract my head, planting my back against the rock wall and facing the mischievous god. "Loki! There must be at least sixty dragons here."

"I-I-I—" He stutters before looking at the ground.

"You are the zmey, aren't you? You stole every one of those dragon eggs." Cautiously I turn my gaze around the corner again and look at the dragons. None of them are chained to the walls or bound in any way. They span a wide array of colors, just like in the dragon wastelands and the dragon stalls at the academy. There are emperor dragons like Elan, and blue dragons like Naga, brown dragons like Drogon, red dragons like Tanda. Seeing each one pulls at my heartstrings. I have not befriended a yellow dragon as of yet, but there are also some of those here as well. They look strikingly like the emperor dragons, and it takes a moment to register that they are yellow, not golden. The dragons roam freely. Except for the occasional roar and burst of flame, they seem to get along quite well. They aren't fighting like the dragons do in the wastelands.

"None of them are chained." The words come out sounding shocked. It's strange to see so many dragons in one enclosed area that aren't forced to be there.

Loki looks up, and his chest puffs out slightly. "Yes. They are all fairly tame and tolerable to anybody who doesn't wish them harm."

"Is that because you raised them from eggs?"

Loki looks at me slyly. "You're still trying to get it out of me, aren't you?"

"Yes. And this seems like evidence that you are the zmey and the one stealing eggs. Clearly, you're not selling them, and you're not killing them. So, what are you doing?"

Loki tosses his hands in the air. "Okay, okay. I'm the zmey. It is one of my shapes, and I assure you these dragons are perfectly safe with me. I'm not harming them in any way"—he holds out a hand in the dragons' direction—"as you can see."

"Then what are you doing with them? Why on earth would you want so many dragons? The food bill must be enormous."

"They hunt for their own food. That's why you saw the dragon flying above earlier. They hide here, where it's warm and they are safe and secure and away from the giants."

"Why would you bring them down to Jotunheim if they could be in danger?"

He runs his pale hand through his shoulder-length black hair. "As I said before, it is my old home. I know my way around here, and I have allies. These allies help me look after the dragons."

"But why take them? Why not leave them in the dragon wastelands? I know the alliance is quite brutal for the dragons, but it is only one egg a year from each breed. If you take the eggs, they become more at risk, as there are fewer to fight off enemies."

Suddenly I hear stomping from the far end of the tunnel. I spin around and look in that direction before facing Loki. "What's that?" I press back against the wall, slipping firmly into a crevice, hoping to blend into the rock wall.

Loki stands in front of me, his legs shoulder-width apart, and spreads his arms out to his sides, remaining fixed as the marching gets closer. I stare at his back, taking in the leather design on his cloak. I'm about to ask again when a group of giants stomps around the corner. I blink and reassess the giants. They look like giants except they are much smaller than I expect. Their faces are pulled into scowls. At first, I think they must be angry, but after studying their mannerisms, I realize it's their regular expression. Their frames are thick, and their heads just peek over the backs of the dragons they lead. Even though the tunnel is much larger than the one on the way to Gilroma's, some of the giants crouch to pass under the low ceiling.

Loki remains standing in front of me as they march past, and he calls to the giants, "Out for the big ride, boys?"

"Training time," one of the giants grunts in response.

"Very good," Loki says. "Train them well."

"Will do, boss," the giant calls over his shoulder.

As the giants pass, I count them—my heart rate rises. There are sixty-one.

The last giant passes and leads his dragon out of the mouth of the cave until I can no longer hear their footsteps in the tunnel.

I scowl and stare at Loki. After seeing the display, it's obvious he is more involved than he made out. "Why are they training?"

Loki doesn't answer me.

"What is the meaning of all these dragons being kept here and giants accompanying them? And why are the giants short?"

Loki's dark eyes land on me. "They are dwarf giants. And the reason there are so many dragons with the giants is because the giants are training them. You just witnessed my army."

- CHAPTER FOUR -

My jaw drops as I look at him. "What do you need an army for?"

Loki scoffs. "Do you honestly think Odin is going to win wars with his attitude toward his people? For instance, consider how he treats wingless Valkyries compared to winged Valkyries. He is so pigheaded, he can't see past his own nose. Just because he's my blood brother and has taken me under his wing doesn't mean I have to agree with his decisions."

"But you're supposed to support him."

"I do." Loki nods slowly. "I do. And I also support my ideas and look after myself."

I indicate the entrance of the caves. "What about the dragons?"

Loki wears an innocent expression. "What about the dragons?"

"They trust you. They trust you to represent them in front of Odin, yet you're stealing their eggs from them in the form of the zmey."

"And your point is?"

"That they trust you, and you're stealing their eggs. It's a conflict of interest."

"How so?"

I let out an aggravated groan. "Because the dragons think that the zmey is harming their eggs. They think you're bringing bad luck to them and hurting their babies." My voice rises to almost a yell.

"That's simply not the case." Loki gestures to where the dragons went as though it explains everything.

"Yes. I can see. But they don't know that, and I still think they might be pretty annoyed."

"Why?"

"Because you're taking their babies without asking. You're using them in a way that they haven't given permission for. What am I supposed to tell them?"

"You don't tell them anything."

I fling my arms out to the sides with agitation. "But they trust me! Now that I know, I have to tell them something about where their babies are going."

"No, you don't. Vanir! If I told Odin everything I know, do you know how much trouble I would be in?"

I roll my eyes and stomp down the tunnel, aiming for the entrance.

Loki's hurried footsteps follow me. "Where are you going?"

"I'm going to watch the dragons to see what you're doing with them."

As Loki's footsteps get closer, I feel the magic well within my body from my pent-up frustration, and it jerks my memory. I spin around to face him. "Why did you mark me when I was trying to protect those eggs?"

"What do you mean?"

I stomp my foot and place my fists on my hips. "Come on, Loki. You know what I mean."

His dark eyes study me for a moment before his shoulders sag. "Yes, yes. Of course I do. I saw you were wingless, and you were so young, yet you stood up to me and stopped me from pinching the dragon eggs. In that instant, I could see your heart was like a lion's, or more like a dragon's. I knew, even back then, that Odin wasn't fair to wingless Valkyries. I disagree with how he treats your kind. The strength I saw in you proved to me that you deserve a better life than being a slave to the winged Valkyries and the gods. I saw that you should be a warrior. So I marked you. I wanted to see what would happen—although you didn't manifest for quite some time, you deserved the special power. I started to think that my marking had failed, but you just needed to grow up a bit. It was a couple of years before you showed any sign of what I had seen in you that day. But even then, no sign of the magic manifested, so I gave it a bit of encouragement as the old woman." He smirks slightly and looks happy with himself.

"I don't know whether to thank you or throttle you. I appreciate that you think I am worth more than Odin and the winged Valkyries give my kind credit for, but you also brought me so much distress. I didn't have a clue what was happening."

"It's not like I could tell you that it was me giving you the power. Otherwise, every wingless Valkyrie would ask for it."

"But then you marked my friends. Why did you mark them?"

"Only because a little birdie told me that that would be helpful."

I frown. "But how? I only told one person before you marked my friends. That was Gilroma, the dark elf I met, but he couldn't have told you because my friends were marked too quickly afterward."

I reach the entrance of the cave and look up into the sky. A dark shadow passes overhead. I watch as a huge yellow dragon flies over, a giant's legs hooked around its neck. Even though these giants are classed as dwarves, they are still much bigger than Valkyries. I feel sorry for the dragons, and I notice that their wing strokes are more labored than when the Valkyries are on their backs.

"Couldn't you have picked a lighter species to sit on the dragons' backs?"

"The giants are outstanding fighters. Even though these are smaller, their size and strength make them better warriors."

I frown, trying to comprehend the information. As I watch the stolen dragons fly overhead, I grieve for the dragon herd's loss, especially the mothers. "Are you going to tell the dragons about their babies?"

Loki shakes his head. "I still don't see why I should."

I expel a breath. "You know that leaves me in a difficult position. I can't guarantee that I won't tell them what's happening. They have been quite upset over the zmey grabbing their eggs. You have stolen a lot."

We stand in silence as we watch the giants and dragons execute their moves, diving and pretending to fight. After a while, Loki asks, "Was there anything else you wanted to ask me? You seemed so insistent on talking to me at Odin's castle."

I shake my head. "I think I've covered everything for now, but I'm still upset about you not telling the dragons." I watch the dragons circle some more and maneuver as they fly higher and change directions with the giants on their backs. "I can see that you're not mistreating the dragons. They look quite healthy and strong, considering the loads they carry. I'm ready to go home now. Are you going to take me back, or is the frost giant going to?"

A smirk spreads across Loki's face. He touches his finger to his chin as if thinking. "Let me see." Suddenly he starts to grow and change shape. His skin changes color until, eventually, he transforms into the blue frost giant that kidnapped me in the first place. He stoops down and holds out his right hand.

I look up into his big eyes. "Seriously, Loki? How many other forms have you taken on? I used to wonder why they call you the god of mischief, but now I'm starting to understand, and you have so many ridiculous forms to hide behind."

The frost giant stands up straight and throws his head back, holding his belly as he lets out a boisterous laugh. I watch as his big belly jumps and jerks up and down. When he finishes laughing, he reaches down and holds out his hand again. I step onto his fingers, and he gently picks me up then carries me back to the entrance of Yggdrasil and climbs the world tree's branches and trunk. Eventually, he arrives at the branch to the world of Asgard. He climbs onto the branch and into Asgard and transforms immediately into the old woman. Even though I know it's one of his shapes, I still find it confusing to see him change into so many different forms.

"That's a strange shape to take. Don't you want to be seen with me?" I'm half-joking, and when I sit, I let out a huff.

"It is best that Odin and his followers do not see you with me. It would only cause trouble for both of us," he says in a husky old voice.

"Actually, I do have one more question."

"Yes?" Loki asks in that same old woman's voice.

"Aren't the giants enemies of Asgard? Yet you're training giants and dragons to fight in the war." I watch him closely as I wait for his answer.

"These particular giants are loyal to me and my cause. Anyway, I must be off."

A feeling of confusion settles over me. I watch the old woman climb up to the tree and disappear into the branches.

- CHAPTER FIVE -

The giant's strides are enormous in comparison to my little ones, making my return to the academy a long walk. I wish Loki could've changed into the giant and carried me back, except he would've been attacked, as frost giants are enemies of Asgard. Becoming impatient, I start to jog. A shadow flies over me, and I look up to see the underbelly of a dragon. Golden scales glimmer, catching the sun's light as she flaps her wings and tilts her head to gaze down at me.

Kara! Elan's voice fills my head as she swoops down and lands in front of me. *I've been so worried about you. Where have you been?*

I shrug and look at her sheepishly. "Let's just say a frost giant kidnapped me."

Her eyes widen with shock. *What?*

I wave a hand at her dismissively. "Don't worry. It was just Loki. He changed into a frost giant and rescued me, well, so he thought, from Mistress Sigrun's punishment. I wanted to talk to him anyway."

Why?

Guilt twists like a knife in my gut as I remember that I haven't told Elan that Loki is the egg-stealing zmey and the one that marked me with magic. Still undecided about whether I should, I think of a quick story. "I wanted to see if he had managed to convince Odin to treat the dragons better and if he had worked out a better alliance with the Valkyrie Academy." I grimace inwardly. It is close to the truth but not really. It was the first thing that came to my mind.

Elan looks at me strangely and tilts her head. *Oh. I'm pretty sure Mother's onto that anyway. I don't know if Odin is budging or not, but we appreciate your effort.* She sniffs me. *You smell different. Where did he take you?*

"He took me to Jotunheim."

The land of the giants?

I nod.

That's weird. Elan sits down on her haunches.

"I know." I try to hide the deception in my voice.

So how come he didn't drop you back at the academy? Dumping you way out here in the wilderness is a bit rude.

"It wasn't like he could transform into a frost giant and drop me off."

Elan chuckles. *No. I can't see that going well.* She stoops in front of me, lowering her shoulders and back. *Here, climb on.*

I gaze up and see my saddle already on her back. "I didn't realize you had this on your back." I tug at the straps, checking their tightness. "It's so hard to see with the scales sewn all over it."

Someone had a good idea.

I had sewn Elan's loose golden scales over the straps and most of the saddle where I didn't sit. I climb on up and hang onto the straps, hooking my feet into the stirrups. Elan stands then crouches before pushing into the sky, and I rise and fall with the beat of her wings. The air is fresh and crisp but nothing like it was in Jotunheim. Goose bumps rise on my skin, and I rub my arms with my hands, trying to warm them up. I could really use my cloak right now.

On Elan's back, it is only a short flight to the academy. She circles and lands on the outskirts close to where she likes to rest when she's not with me. Instantly two winged Valkyries fly our way. Elan blocks their path to me and snarls.

I move next to Elan's head and rest my hand on her snout. "It's okay, Elan. Relax. They were probably sent here by Mistress Sigrun to see why I haven't turned up for my punishment."

All the more reason to tear them apart. Elan's voice sounds like she spoke through gritted teeth even though she communicated to me telepathically.

"Seriously, it's okay." I rub her snout some more.

"Kara!" The two Valkyries thump down on the ground beside us, and I look at them properly, realizing that it is Rota and Prima. Rota's face is wan, and I catch a sorrowful look in her eyes before she glances at the ground.

Prima crosses her arms over her chest. "You're late! Mistress Sigrun demands your immediate presence."

I shrug. "I kind of got kidnapped. It wasn't exactly my fault."

"You're still late. There's no excuse for that. You should never leave the mistress waiting." Prima waves her index finger at me.

Oh, dragon scales! Elan rolls her eyes. *The same old rubbish all the time.*

Prima grabs me by my arm, and Rota joins her, mouthing, "Sorry," when Prima can't see her.

I shake them off lightly. "There's no need for that. I'm coming anyway."

Reluctantly they release me, but their eyes never leave me as they march me inside the academy.

I'm here if you need me, Elan says telepathically as we pass through the doors. *Just say the word.*

The two Valkyries march me toward Mistress Sigrun's office, down the hall past the dining room.

Hilda calls out, "Kara! You're okay!" She looks at Rota and Prima, narrowing her eyes at Rota. "Well, sort of."

They knock harshly on the door, and a gruff voice calls out, "Come in." They barge into the room, pushing me forward before them.

"We found her." Prima's voice is full of pride.

Mistress Sigrun gazes up for her paperwork. "About time." Her eyes constrict as she looks at me. "You're late."

"Sorry, Mistress. I was kidnapped." I add the slightest bit of sarcasm to my tone, knowing that it won't make any difference.

She rolls her eyes. "You'll say anything to get out of work and punishment."

I hold my tongue, mainly because if I don't, I know that I'll be in more trouble.

"Odin is displeased with you, and he has requested that I punish you severely academy-style. I have put you through many trials and wars in the past. None of them seem to have achieved the desired result. You have disgraced us time and time again. This time you will be put in your place."

Silently, I await my fate, not sure what she will bestow upon me.

After a few moments, she says, "There is another war on Midgard. This one is of a large scale. Many warriors are falling, and the senior Valkyries are having trouble keeping up with all the souls. We're about to disembark and help them with their challenge, and you're coming with us."

I frown in confusion. This is supposed to be a punishment, yet she is taking me to Midgard. "As much as I want to help, what am I supposed to do there, Mistress? I cannot reap souls."

"You'll find out once we get there," she snaps. "I'm sure we'll find something for you to do."

"Can I bring my dragon?"

She scowls. "No, you definitely cannot. This is your punishment. You have to deal with it on your own. You shouldn't even use your magic, but I'm sure you will."

I feel disheartened knowing that I can't take Elan.

"Right. Let's get going. I've received the internal call."

- CHAPTER SIX -

I frown. I haven't heard of an internal alarm
for Midgard before. Perhaps it is a secret thing
that the winged Valkyries know about. None of
it matters anyway because I don't have a
choice. I'm still going to Midgard. Rota and
Prima escort me down the hall to my room and
stand outside the door as I grab my weapons,
securing my quiver of arrows over my back
along with my bow and sliding my sword's

sheath between my back and the quiver. I then tuck my sling strap onto my back pants pocket.

When I exit my room, Rota is gone, and Mist is in her place.

"Where's Rota?"

"Oh, I didn't want to miss this opportunity, so I swapped with her."

I hadn't thought such an evil smile could occupy a such pretty face before. As I look at Mist, I realize I was wrong.

"Enough questions." Roughly Prima grabs me and accompanies me every step of the way with Mist flanking my other side. They handle me as though I'm a prisoner. This puzzles me, as I have spent years trying to prove myself and gain access to Midgard. Now they are acting as though I'm not going to come. It makes me think that it's not going to be a simple trip, that Mistress Sigrun has something else planned. If Rota were here, I could have tried to ask her, if I had the opportunity, but it probably would have been impossible with Prima remaining so near.

Mist shoves me, a malicious look on her face, which makes me wish I could take Elan. I would feel safer for whatever Mistress Sigrun has in store.

Mist and Prima march me down the hallway of the academy, and the second we reach the exit, they grab me on either side, carrying me between them as they fly up the mountain to Heimdall's post.

"Good day, Valkyries." The big gatekeeper's eyes show hints of sadness as he faces me. "So, you finally get to go to Midgard again, young Valkyrie."

I nod. "Although I don't know why they have to escort me."

"Just remember, you are going to land in a place where enemies are numerous. Be wary. Especially without your dragon to accompany you." He glances from Prima to Mist, his face expressionless, then back to me. "The dangers may be unexpected."

"What are you talking about?" I try to read his expression. I'm not sure if I see worry on his face.

"That you should be wary. Never let your guard down on any side."

We follow him inside his portal post, and he turns the handle, filling the area with rainbow colors moments before we are sucked through its portal and down to Midgard. My stomach lurches with the motion. Even though it's not my first time, my stomach still isn't used to the vortex of the Bifrost.

My feet hit the ground, and my legs collapse underneath me, slamming my hip on the ground. Pain shoots down my leg. Before I get a chance to roll over and rub my hip, I'm yanked up by the two Valkyries and pulled into the air as they fly to our destination with me slinging in between them.

I gaze across the land of Midgard, and I'm still stunned by its beauty. The skies are a clear blue, and the greenery of the trees and grass contrast nicely in the valley and surrounding the rivers. Pushing aside the awkwardness of swinging between the two winged Valkyries, I search the land for any sign of the battlefield. I can't find it. From my experience, it is often very close to the Bifrost portal.

"Where are you taking me?" I ask Prima.

Her eyes narrow. "Don't speak to me." She turns and looks in the other direction.

"I was only asking where you are taking me." My mind wanders to the sword slung on my back that Rota fixed for me, and at the same time adding wings to the sides of my hilt as an emblem. If only Prima and Mistress Sigrun could see what I was trying to do and show me some support. It would make my life so much easier.

As though reading my thoughts, Prima says, "I don't know what you've done to Rota. But she refused to take you here, so Mist offered instead."

I look at Mist in time to see her pull a hair clip out of her pocket and slide it into her hair. After fiddling with it for a few moments, she gazes at her fingernails. "Yes. You're such a burden." She rolls her eyes. "No matter what happens today, I hope we never have to bring you back."

"Nice." I don't hide the sarcasm in my voice. "After everything I've done to protect the winged Valkyries."

"You've done nothing to protect us." Mist's tone is spiteful. "All you've managed to do is mess up our hair and break a couple of our fingernails. And for that, you should be punished."

We sink lower, and I search the ground. No one is on the field below. "Where are all the warriors? I was supposed to be here to help out with the influx of warriors."

"Is that so?" Prima asks. "Perhaps we're here to see if you are a warrior."

I frown. "What do you mean?"

"You'll see," Mist says, twirling her long blond locks with her free hand.

Realizing that they aren't going to tell me what's going on, I hold my questions and keep my eyes open, silently gathering my magic, just in case. I'm getting the sense that this may be a trap of some sort. It's not the first time Mistress Sigrun has played unfairly.

Prima and Mist unceremoniously dump me on the ground then take off. Pushing off the grass, I turn around and watch them leave. A cloud of confusion fogs my thoughts. I don't understand why they are leaving me in a place with no soldiers. It's an empty field.

The magic wells impatiently inside me, sizzling in my palms. It is at the point of taking over if I don't grab control. Absentmindedly, I reach up and grab the necklace that Gilroma gave me the other day. As my hand touches the blue stone, something sizzles out of my palm involuntarily, and it shoots into the rock. The stone warms and glows for a moment before dying down.

I stare at the necklace, holding it between my forefinger and thumb. It looks the same, but I swear something just happened, even though there's no evidence of it now. I spin the necklace around. It's a beautiful stone that, so far, has done nothing for me. Now, all of a sudden, it seems to have taken some of my magic. I felt the surge as it left me, and the bright light shot through the stone. Gilroma had said it would help me channel my magic in a way other than just through my hands, but so far, nothing has happened. It's been nothing but a pretty necklace.

A noise behind me catches my attention. I drop the necklace and spin around. I had forgotten where I was for a moment. I let my guard down while distracted by the necklace.

I search for the cause of the noise and come up empty. In the trees across the field, something crashes, and my eyes dart to the position. Leaves rustle, and branches sway as something makes its way through the shrubbery. As I stare at the spot, a sea of black emerges from the bushes and onto the open field. Pale faces and black wings and bodies dressed in black attire walk out, exposing themselves, slowly heading in my direction. There are so many of them. They are all angels of death, and their faces wear grim expressions.

I study each one of them, looking for my friend, but I can't see Harut anywhere. Perhaps if I find him, he can tell me what's going on because I'm confused. There are no warriors anywhere in sight, yet here comes a small army of angels of death, and they don't look happy. All their eyes are focused on me. I have no idea what has gotten into these males, but I guess I'm about to find out. They are still some distance away, and I glance over my shoulder.

Perhaps winged Valkyries will approach behind me as a group to face off with the angels of death invading Midgard.

As I gaze over my shoulder, all that I see is open space. There is not a winged Valkyrie in sight. And there is no Elan that I can call upon because she's not even in this realm. My knees shake as I realize I'm about to face this whole army of winged angels of death on my own with no way to escape.

- CHAPTER SEVEN -

As the army of good-looking males swarm my way, their faces become more distinct. I recognize the angel of death who had called Harut away from me last time I saw him. His hair is longer, falling to his shoulders, and somehow, he looks broader, as though he's been working out and practicing his fighting. He seems just as unimpressed to see me as he did the last time.

An icy chill runs down my spine as I observe each angel of death's face. I have no idea why I'm in their focus or why the winged Valkyries have left me in this field to face them alone. I'm not sure if they are going to attack me. Perhaps, by some miracle, they just want to talk. The look on their faces tells me a different story.

Four angels of death land around me, boxing me in on all sides. I'm trapped in a way that represents a street-style mugging. My skin crawls with unease as I observe each one. Their faces are etched with concentration and signs that they are ready to attack.

One of the angels behind me calls, "Awaiting your order, Cael."

Instinctively, my body moves into a ready stance with my feet shoulder-width apart and my arms relaxed by my sides. My ears and eyes are on full alert, watching every movement and sound around me. The minutes tick by, seeming like hours as I wait for something to happen. I gaze back at the main angel of death. He nods to the angel behind me who had called to him, and his long black hair trails behind him as he approaches, aided by the breeze.

Cael stops in front of me, his stance agile and ready to react. "Ah. The enemy of my enemy yet not my ally."

I remain in my ready stance and stare at him, confused. He stands outside the square of angels of death surrounding me. Cael then paces around the group that holds me captive, as though stalking his prey.

"Why am I here?" I ask. "I don't understand what I've done to be given this kind of attention."

His dark-brown eyebrow rises in an arch as he peers at me and paces slowly around my four guards. "Did your mistress not tell you?"

"Mistress didn't tell me anything." I turn on the spot, watching his every move. "But there's nothing unusual about that."

One side of his mouth lifts in a half smile. "You have been delivered as a trade."

"Really? I don't believe I signed an agreement."

Cael throws his head back and chuckles. "Like you have a choice." He looks at the guards surrounding me. "Seize her!"

All four angels dive toward me, and my arms are secured by my sides as one grabs me around the torso. Instantly my defense reflexes kick in. I slam my heel on the angel's toes, relax my knees, and let my body drop. At the same time, I twist and slam my elbow into his ribs. The arms that secured me release their grip, and I dive out of their embrace. Another angel tries to grab me by my arms. I swing around, yanking myself free before he can secure his hold, and I hit him in the face. As his head flings backward, someone grabs my hand from the side. I twist my wrist, loosening the grip, then flick off their hold and spin to kick the angel in the head.

Another secures a handful of my hair near the skin, and pain sears through my scalp. I slam my hand over the fingers seizing my hair, crushing them on my head. Tilting my head down while bending his wrist, I yank him forward. He stumbles, and I kick him in the knee. A crack reaches my ears, and he lets go of my hair, crying out in pain, with his knee bent in the wrong direction.

The attacks continue from all sides. A replacement angel takes the place of the one with the broken knee, and the main angel of death keeps watching.

A mixture of magic and anger wells within me, and I long to release them. But with every attack, the angels' grips get tighter and give me less room to move. I wriggle and squirm and fight back as much as I can, feeling the magic within me dying to escape. It's almost as though the angels of death can feel my power because each attack is an attempt to secure my arms, inhibiting me from releasing my magic with my hands. Each physical struggle drains my energy, leaving me with fewer chances to build more magic. I wriggle and squirm some more, trying desperately to release my hands, and envision being able to set my magic free.

A spot on my chest suddenly grows warm with deep, intense heat. I gaze down, and the necklace Gilroma gave me catches my eye. At first, I think it is the rays of the sun catching on the stone until suddenly a burst of light shoots out and collides with the angel of death in front of me, knocking him to the ground. I trace the direction that he stumbled, and my eyes widen when I spot him lying still and looking unconscious. I look up in shock, trying to remain alert, ready for the next attack. I don't have to wait long before another darts in. The angels of death must have a vendetta against me to brush off their worry for a comrade so easily.

I hear a grunt, and something darts at me from the side, grabbing my arms from behind. I wriggle within the grasp, unable to free myself. I slam my foot back onto the toes of the assailant. A cry of agony sounds in my ear, and long, dark strands of hair tickle my shoulder. Cael has joined my attackers. His arms release me slightly, and I spin around to face him, the stench of corpses catching in my throat.

"What do you want from me?" I ask through gritted teeth. "I have done nothing to you or your kind. I can't even reap souls. So, what is your problem?"

He straightens slightly and looks at me strangely. "Do you mean besides the fact that I hate your kind?"

"I don't believe you've had anything to do with my kind until I showed up. If you mean the winged Valkyries, then that is different. As you can see, I don't have wings." I step back and cross my arms. "The only interactions I've had with your kind were with Harut, who has always been kind to me. I don't understand why you're attacking me."

Cael sneers. "Harut is nothing but a show pony who glides in and out when he feels like it. His loyalty to our kind is not yet proven."

I frown. "I don't know what you're talking about. But it sounds like an argument that is between your kind. I still don't understand what you want from me."

One of the four corner guards darts at me from behind to grab me. I pick up his movement just in time to stand slightly to the side, squat, and throw him over my shoulder. He lands on the ground in front of me with a thud. I look down at him, proud of my achievement. I hadn't done that maneuver for quite some time and barely had a chance to practice it. His wide, dark eyes stare at me with surprise.

"We were told you would come in peace." Cael casts a disgruntled look at the fallen attacker.

"By whom?" I ask.

"By your mistress. We have traded many good warrior souls from the next battle to capture you."

"What?" I don't hide my surprise. "Your warrior souls are just as important to you as the Valkyries' warrior souls are to them. You fight the Valkyries constantly over the souls. Why would I be worth the trade of several of your souls to the Valkyries? It just doesn't make sense."

"Our goddess, Freya, would like to see you." Cael seems to be in pain as he says these words.

Both my eyebrows rise. "What? Why would she want to see me?"

His shoulders slump in resignation. "That is something you will have to ask her. It is her decision and has nothing to do with me."

"And you say that the Valkyries are going to receive several of your souls to train for Ragnarök?" I ask.

He nods, looking sad. "That was the agreement, though I don't understand why. Still, I will honor it because that is what our goddess wants despite that it goes against every fiber of my being."

As much as I don't trust this angel of death and don't see any signs of Harut, I weigh the fact that the Valkyries will receive several souls from the next battle, more than what they usually would, because of the agreement with the angels of death. Purely because of this, I say, "Take me away."

- CHAPTER EIGHT -

Again I am grabbed by the arms and hoisted into the air. Being carried around by winged beings other than dragons is starting to get on my nerves, but I force myself to remember that it's for a good cause. I may not physically be able to reap souls for Valhalla, but this can be my contribution. I still don't understand why a trade-off of one wingless Valkyrie is worth several souls to Valhalla.

After flying a few miles, they land, and Cael pulls a long piece of black material out of his pocket. He lifts it and aims for my eyes.

I pull my head back. "What are you doing?"

"You need to be blindfolded."

I scowl. "Are you serious? I'm coming of my own free will. Why would I need to be blindfolded?"

"Our location is a secret. Nobody in the known realms is aware of exactly where we live, and we regularly change our location."

"You've got to be kidding me."

He shakes his head. "No. Freya is all for peace and love. And the moment our location is discovered, we attract bad attention. Then we have to move again."

I frown. "But you guys fight us. That is not peaceful."

"We only fight for the souls to help protect us and bring us harmony, and Freya loves a good-looking warrior with a big heart."

I gaze at each of the angels of death. They hold a distinct handsomeness, in their own way, but unlike the Valkyries, they each look unique. "Aren't you guys that? The majority of your kind are quite attractive—besides the stench—and you're good, strong warriors. Wouldn't you be what she wants?"

"We are not her type. She requires a human." With the material slung between his hands, Cael reaches up toward my face. This time I allow him to secure it over my eyes. Once the blindfold is yanked tight, I feel myself being lifted again. The pressure on my shoulders makes them throb as we fly in whichever direction they are taking me. By the time my feet hit the ground, my arms ache from being hauled through the air. As I'm set down, I stumble, unable to see where to place my feet. Strong hands capture me and stop me from falling.

"Was the blindfold really necessary?"

When my feet are steady, the strong hands release me and yank off my blindfold.

It takes a while for my eyes to adjust until, finally, they focus on the friendly face of Harut. He smiles, and a strange tingling sensation courses through my body, almost causing my knees to buckle. My body's response brings Eir's remarks to mind. Perhaps she is right. Maybe I have a greater interest in him than friendship. Feeling my cheeks warm at the thought, I do my best to push my feelings aside.

Harut reaches forward and embraces me. "Kara. It's good to see you."

Trying to calm my excited heart, I breathe in deeply then quickly plug my nose over his shoulder. It's such a shame that the angels of death smell like corpses. I guess it would be a good reason for Freya to not have an interest in taking them as romantic partners.

I breathe through my mouth. "It's great to see you too. Do you know what's going on or why I'm here?"

"I don't know. Leave it with me, and I'll look into it. In the meantime, I'll make sure you're looked after."

"Thanks." The weight on my shoulders lifts slightly.

Despite Harut being here to assist me, I am still trapped in an unknown land. He pushes off from the ground and leaves me. Instantly, the loneliness closes in.

I'm grabbed and dragged roughly past many small buildings then much bigger buildings made up of a few rooms joined together. The small stone houses stand relatively close together, giving the impression of a town.

I glare at the angel of death handling me. "Where are you taking me?"

"Freya is not ready to see you, so you must be escorted to an enclosed room." He yanks my arm, and we head toward a building a few yards away. He opens the door and pushes me inside, slamming the door behind us. He grabs cuffs chained to the wall and secures them around my wrists and secures another set around my ankles.

I glance around at the windowless walls and huff. "This is like a mini-dungeon. It's a bit rude to trap me in here when I came of my own free will." I rattle the chains secured to my wrists. "So why are you chaining me and locking me up?"

"I wouldn't call it free will if you're getting traded for several souls." He shoots me an annoyed glance. "So you're still being locked up."

He shoves me, and I stumble backward, tripping over my feet and chains, and fall on my backside. Looking satisfied, he exits the building and slams the door behind him. The walls rattle slightly, jingling the keys hanging on the wall across the room. Instantly they have my attention. I find it strange that they left the keys inside the room. They must be confident that I can't get to them.

I focus on the keys and pool my magic. Perhaps I will be able to use it to unhook the keys and bring them to me.

Narrowing my focus, I concentrate on my magic, letting it gather. Even though I'm here of my own free will, I don't appreciate being chained up like this. It certainly doesn't make me feel like a welcome guest. Their treatment of me leads me to think they want to harm me. At the same time, Freya asked to see me, so I hope that means that she doesn't want me dead or injured. And even though the angels of death don't trust me, and Valkyries are their enemies, they shouldn't harm me, because they respect Freya's rules and requests. My mind travels to Harut. It puzzles me that he wasn't with the other angels of death when they came to grab me.

The door handle rattles, capturing my attention, and interrupts the summoning of my magic. Cael walks in.

"What is this place?" I ask. "This one little area has so many buildings. Is it a common practice for you all to live in one spot?"

"This is an academy for the angels of death. So I guess you're kind of a rare visitor," he says.

"Wait, so you also have angels of death in training?"

"Yes."

"But I didn't see many senior angels of death or at least none older than you are."

"I am one of the instructors and teachers."

"But you look so young."

"That's because angels of death are also cursed with long lives and youthful looks, just like the Valkyries. It's one of the ways they keep their warriors fit and healthy."

Before I can let this register, I am hauled to my feet, and the angel of death grabs the keys off the wall, unlocks my cuffs, and calls for the assistance of two other angels. They handle me harshly, securing my arms behind my back.

I know I can struggle and weave my way out of their grasp, but I don't see the point. "You don't have to grasp me so firmly, you know. I'm curious to see why Freya wants to see me, which means I won't be escaping."

Cael studies my face. A strong breeze blows from behind him, pushing his hair into his eyes, and he pushes it back. After a moment, he looks at the two angels securing me on both sides and waves his hand, indicating for them to release their grip on me, which makes for a much more comfortable walk.

They march me through open fields covered in beautiful green grass and shrubs, reminding me of Midgard. In the distance, I spot a castle standing tall, with a warrior standing guard at each of the ramparts.

The angels of death march me up the steps to the entrance, and we're granted access immediately by the guards standing watch.

Impressive water fountains decorate the large hall, displays of strong warriors with bare-muscled torsos carrying heavy loads, and water pouring over them.

I ogle them as we pass through the hall and into the throne room. Off to the side of the throne is a daybed occupied by three warriors, and a beautiful woman draped across their laps. She giggles as they feed her grapes from a dangling bunch. The blue fabric of her long, flowing dress drapes over her curves perfectly, showing off the contours of her body. One bare-chested warrior runs his fingers through her beautiful blond hair.

Her head turns when she hears us in the doorway, showing off her perfect blue eyes. Slowly she moves into a sitting position and watches as we enter the room. She wriggles her hips between the legs of the warriors and sits beside them. She observes me closely as the angels of death march me forward. Her voice contains no malice as she says, "Kara. Welcome!"

- CHAPTER NINE -

My feet are glued to the floor as she moves toward me. Her movements are sensual and mesmerizing, and the material of her dress sways with the flow of her hips. I should be used to seeing beings as beautiful as she is, but none have matched her splendor—not even the impeccable features of the Valkyries. Her soft shoes barely make a sound as she crosses the marble floor. When she nears, she holds out a pale flawless hand and clasps mine graciously. She steps back and appraises me from head to toe.

Her hand slides slowly up my arm, and she twirls the ends of my long, dark hair before stroking her hand along my cheek. "Such beauty. I've heard of your lovely features and this raven hair." She tosses it slightly aside, and it droops gracefully past my shoulder. She turns and faces the warriors lying beside her throne. "Isn't she beautiful, great warriors?"

The one in the middle, with his white shirt parted to his waist, speaks. "True, my lady. But none are as beautiful as you."

She turns and smiles, looking satisfied with the answer.

"My lady, why did you wish to see me?" I curtsy slightly, not knowing what else to do.

"Rumors of a young Valkyrie without wings that is stirring trouble across the land of Asgard. My angels have confirmed these rumors. Some are not pleased." She raises an eyebrow as she glances at the three angels of death surrounding me. "I hear the winged Valkyries are also displeased."

I let out a groan, and my shoulders droop. "I only wish to do my part to help save Asgard and become a valuable member."

"And a valuable member you are." She paces around the back of me, running her long fingers across my quiver still attached to my back and plucking playfully at a couple of my arrow shafts. "I have heard many great things."

"Thank you, my lady." I frown. "But I still don't understand why you wanted to see me."

She tosses a hand. "It is true that I haven't cared much for Valkyries in the past. They are such violent beings. I understand that they are that way because they are following Odin's orders and trying to raise an army for Valhalla and Ragnarök. But then I heard a few rumors that you also want peace. Peace amongst your own kind for a start and peace between the dragons and the Valkyries, and I wouldn't be surprised if your peace wishes extend further than that."

She pulls at the hilt of my sword, and my nerves fire when I hear metal sliding. I brace myself, ready to defend myself, but the sound stops a split second after it starts. Keeping her hand on the hilt of my sheathed sword, Freya walks around to face me, her expression filled with amusement. She drops the handle, and it slides back into its sheath. "I am amused that you wear these impressive weapons, yet you came peacefully for a Valkyrie. At the same time, I hear you are not afraid to fight. Fight for what you believe is right. Whether it be with words or actions."

I think long and hard for a moment. "Most of my actions were to prove the worth of myself as a wingless Valkyrie and the other wingless Valkyries, but the dragons decided to get involved as well. I want to say they are responsible for how I have grown fond of them and other creatures. But I did call attention to myself the day I saved the dragon leader's egg from the zmey. I guess, if you think about it, you can call that a step toward peace. But I am not the peaceful one. I would say Eir, one of my close friends, is the one who likes to help uphold peace."

Her brow puckers. "I have not heard of her."

"Have you not heard of the wingless Valkyries who fight alongside me?"

She looks over her shoulder at one of the warriors sitting on the bench. He nods. She turns back to face me. "I guess I have, but only your name was mentioned."

"But I still don't understand why you called me here."

She smiles knowingly and clasps her hands in front of her. "I've heard rumors of another growing army. I believe they might cause trouble."

"What kind of army? And from where?" I ask. "Is it in Asgard?"

She shakes her head, and her blond curls bounce near her face. "No. I don't believe it's in Asgard."

"Perhaps you mean the dark elves that attacked us not so long ago."

She looks thoughtful for a moment, bringing her long, dainty forefinger to her mouth and lightly tapping her lips. After a while, she shakes her head. "No, I don't believe it is the dark elves. There's a rumor of another army. I believe it may be based out of Jotunheim."

I gasp, doing my best to look surprised. "In the land of the giants? And you think this army might be up to no good?"

She taps her forefinger a few more times against her lips. "Yes. I believe they may be up to no good. Have you heard of anything coming from there?"

I study her flawless features. She is stunning on the outside and has a trustworthy face, but deep down, I know that I've not met her before and can't be sure of her intentions. Nor do I know what Loki's plans are with the army of dragons and dwarf giants. Neither has shown hostility toward me other than the angels of death apprehending me. As neither party has my complete trust, I decide to keep the knowledge to myself. "I haven't heard of this army you are talking about. Is your source to be trusted?"

She looks thoughtful for a moment longer. "I believe so. They haven't let me down in the past. It may only be stories, but if you hear of anything, let me know."

"And how will I do that?"

A thoughtful expression crosses her face then lightens. "I will give you this." She pulls something out of her blouse and grabs my hand and opens it, placing the item on my palm. I catch my breath. It is a silver charm of two wings with a trumpet lying over the top. "It's beautiful," I gush as I rub it between my fingers.

She chuckles and closes my palm. "Please refrain from rubbing it unless you have something to tell me. I know you can't hear it, but the sound I hear when it is rubbed is very high-pitched."

My cheeks tingle with embarrassment. "Sorry."

"It's fine. Just remember, if you hear of anything, this will call me and alert me the second you rub it. After I am alerted, somehow, I'll get in touch with you, and we will discuss it. If you hear anything of an army, whether it be good or bad, let me know."

I open my hand and gaze down at the wings then back at her. "Okay. Will you also let me know if you hear anything? Forgive me for being so direct, but if you discover significant information, I would like to know."

Her blue eyes look at me under a cocked eyebrow. "You are as headstrong as they say. You definitely are a challenge to gods and goddesses, even if you are only a Valkyrie."

I bow my head, feeling slightly guilty. I gaze at the ground, then a thought crosses my mind, and I look purposefully into her blue eyes. "I only challenge a god or goddess when I wish to know more or I'm looking for some proof. Forgive me for my brazenness, but I think trust should go both ways, and seeing as you are not my immediate goddess, I will question and request some information in return."

She briefly stares at me in silence then suddenly bursts out laughing. "I was only toying with you. If I hear anything that will help toward peace, I will certainly let you know. But I expect the same in exchange."

I nod my head. "Of course."

"Until next time." She grabs my hand, squeezes it, then lets it drop to my side. With a graciousness I have not encountered before, she sways her hips on her way to her throne.

I unhook my quiver and attach the charm to its side, almost missing the hook when someone nudges me harshly from the side. I glance up to see the dark eyes of Cael prodding me forward. When I don't move instantly, he nudges me again, nods his head toward the door, and grunts.

I roll my eyes. "You know, I understand more when you use your words. There is no need to be brutal or harsh." I gaze back at the goddess, who strokes the face of an innocent-looking warrior. Then I turn back to the angel of death. "Are you sure you work for her?"

Cael grabs my arm and shoves me forward. We march out of the throne room, through the stone corridors, and out into the beautiful surroundings. He directs me back to the camp where the angels of death had held me before. We stand outside the building where I had been imprisoned, and the senior member of the angels of death stands in front of me. His long black hair whips angrily in the wind, matching the expression on his face.

"You may go." Cael turns as if to leave.

"And how may I go? I don't know how I got here in the first place."

He turns, and he looks as though he's about to say something snarky to the two angels of death on either side of me, when he is interrupted by a voice off to my right.

"I'll take her."

- CHAPTER TEN -

I glance to the right and see Harut jogging toward me, his eyes set with determination, giving his face an intensely powerful look and making him more endearing. Already I can feel my cheeks burn as his deep, dark eyes study my face.

He grabs my hand, and his touch is sensually warm yet cold at the same time. He is standing downwind, and without the smelly distraction, my intense feelings make it hard to function properly. My stomach whirls when he gently pulls me forward.

"Come, Kara. Let's go." He coaxes me away from the circle of angels of death and the area of their academy. Then he pulls a long piece of black material out of his pocket.

"Why do you all have one of those in your pocket?" Despite having an idea of what the material is going to be used for, I can't help but think how odd it is that he carries one, and my mouth turns up in a smile.

"I don't want to use this, Kara, but we're forced to keep this place a secret, and I stick by the rules."

I look into his apologetic eyes. He has shown nothing but kindness to me, and I don't believe that will change. He closes in and places the material over my eyes. His chest rubs against my arm as he moves to tie the knot securely at the back of my head. I release a contented sigh then remember myself and still my breath. I remind myself that even though he is kind to me, the angels of death are classed as enemies of the Valkyries because of our fight to reap the warriors' souls. Once the knot is tightened, his hand runs down my arm until it grabs my hand, and pleasant tingles linger on my skin. I become aware of the absence of another set of hands, and I suddenly remember that I was carried by two angels of death to get here.

"How are you going to get me out of here? I'll be too heavy for you to carry."

"I have my ways." The back of his hand brushes against my chest, and he scoops the necklace Gilroma gave me into his palm. A delighted shiver runs down my body.

"I believe this is filled with magic."

Instinctively, I reach up for the necklace, and my fingers brush his. I flinch, ready to pull away, but choose to leave my hand there, facing my fears. "How did you know that?"

"I have my sources." His voice is deep and warm. "I need you to hold on to the necklace and concentrate on being as light as a feather so I can lift you up and carry you along with me."

I close my fingers around the necklace. "I've never done this before."

"Believe in yourself, and believe in your magic. Picture yourself floating, being light, and then it will be okay."

I concentrate hard on floating, working hard on quieting my racing mind, wondering how he knows this. Eventually, the ground vanishes from under my feet, and I have the sensation of being lifted. Harut's grasp on my arm tightens, and he pulls, the sensation coming in waves, like the rise and fall of beating wings. I trust him to take me back to where I will be safe and finally home. Panic sets in for a moment. I don't know how Harut is going to get past Heimdall's post and into Asgard. I still my mind. He is probably just going to drop me off where the Bifrost channels to Asgard.

The rise and fall of his wings are calming, almost mesmerizing. The atmosphere changes, and it doesn't smell or feel like Midgard anymore. Instead, it feels more like home, which I didn't think he would be able to enter. I feel my body lower slowly until my feet hit the ground.

"We're here. Did you enjoy your flight?" A hint of amusement infuses his voice.

"I think it would have been nicer if I could have seen where I was going."

The soft touch of his hand brushes my cheek, and my lips part with a gasp. Something warm and wet presses against them, and my cheeks burn as I realize he must be kissing me. I suck in a breath, stunned, and then choke on the sudden intake, coughing and spluttering off to the side.

My gosh! Kara! There you are. Elan's voice penetrates my thoughts, distracting me from what just happened. *Did I really just see that?* The ground vibrates with a thud when she lands not far from me. *Who is this you're kissing?*

I frown. "You've met Harut before."

Oh no. It's definitely not Harut.

I yank the blindfold from my eyes, and when they focus, I'm confronted with a weird and ugly face. Glowing yellow eyes observe me. "Gilroma?"

I want to scrub my lips and spit. Instead, I turn my head and discreetly rub my lips on my shoulder. I don't understand. Harut was the one who brought me back to Asgard.

Elan moves closer to Gilroma, dropping her nose to sniff him.

Gilroma eyes her briefly then turns and studies me curiously. "I could sense a presence entering Asgard."

Yeah, that's not all you could sense. Elan's voice is full of cheek.

"Elan!" A different kind of embarrassment settles over me.

She tilts her head to the side and stares at me with a funny face. *Just saying it the way it is.*

My cheeks burn.

Where have you been anyway? she asks. *And who is this guy?*

"This is Gilroma. The dark elf I wanted you to meet the other day from the cave under the mountain."

So this is the elusive Gilroma from the cave. She raises an eyebrow. *You two were certainly looking cozy.* She chuckles.

With confusion, I look at Gilroma. "Did you kiss me? Is she telling the truth?"

"I think she's teasing you."

I glance from Elan to Gilroma. I have no idea what to believe.

"Where have you been anyway?" Gilroma asks.

"That's a long story. Apparently, I've popped up on another goddess's radar."

Elan settles down on her haunches and stares at Gilroma before her eyes move to me. *Kara. I'm not sure I trust this guy. Can I eat him?*

A huff of air escapes my mouth, and I gawk at her. "No!"

Gilroma looks at us in confusion.

Aww! You always take the fun out of things. She slumps down, resting her belly on the ground.

I scowl at her. "It's not negotiable." I want to say more, but I know anything I say Gilroma will be able to hear.

Elan pouts, sticking out her bottom lip before lying on her side. *Okay. I guess I can leave him alone for a while.*

"Good."

Honestly, where have you been all this time?

"It's a long story, Elan. How about we go for a long ride so we can speak for a bit?"

Sure. I have some things to tell you anyway, she says.

I look back at Gilroma. "Thanks for checking on me."

Elan already has my saddle on her back, a habit she has picked up recently in case she needs to get me out of trouble. I climb on Elan's back and look down at him. His eyes carry a strange expression.

"Don't worry. I'll be fine. Elan always looks after me. Don't you, Elan?" I stroke the side of her neck.

Of course I do. She pushes into the air, and I gaze down at Gilroma. His eyes don't leave us until we disappear.

We fly high, and the wind turns icy as we ascend. My face burns from the cold. I reach down into the new pouch I made and attached to my saddle, and I pull out my cloak. I thread my arms through the sleeves and pull the hood over my head. Instantly the cool breeze is blocked out, and cozy warmth builds within my cloak.

Elan's scales disappear underneath me, and I know that I will also be invisible. This thought brings me comfort after what I just went through, knowing that it would be hard for anyone to kidnap me or bestow me with the scrutiny of Mistress Sigrun's punishment. I always feel safe under Elan's care.

We fly for a while, and the rise and fall of her wing beats lull me to sleep after an exhausting day. After some time, Elan's voice invades my dreams. *I have something to tell you.*

I sit up straight with a start. "Sorry, Elan. I fell asleep. What do you have to tell me?"

Mother has decided to help us more. She is going to step in and talk to some of the vicious dragons in the stalls. Hopefully, she can convince them to trust the wingless Valkyries. She is trying this tactic first, and if she doesn't succeed, she may hand over more younglings.

My tiredness is pushed away by my excitement. "Really? That's great!"

It's only for the wingless Valkyries, not for the winged. She still doesn't trust them. Odin has also promised to keep his hands off the dragons. It took a lot of fighting, and eventually, he agreed that the dragons associating with the wingless Valkyries is a good thing for building relationships. He said he'll keep this agreement as long as no dragons attack Asgard or the Valkyries or any of his warriors. I don't know how she did it, but it's a step forward.

I lean forward and stroke her scales along her neck. "This is great news!"

And the other good news is that Ness has been watching Tanda's interaction with Britta from a distance and how you, Hildr, and Eir interact with the dragons. Because of this, she is willingly giving up her babies to be cared for by the wingless Valkyries.

"Really? That's great! And how did Eingana have this conversation with Odin?"

Through Loki, as per usual.

My breath catches at the mention of his name and his recent association with the dragons. "Elan."

Yes?

"There is something I have to tell you. I had to find out the truth before I could pass the information on to you. Even then, I was asked to keep this a secret, but I can't keep it from you."

What is it?

"It's about the dragon eggs. I found out where they are going."

The End

Besieged: Book 9 is released in January, 2020.

ACKNOWLEDGMENTS

I am touched by the enormous amount of support I have received from my immediate family. My husband has been a helpful first reader and at times been a wonderful motivator, with hints of ideas to help me through the blanks. The support from my three sons has also been overwhelming. They have put up with my head being in the clouds, thinking about the next plot twist or story for several years. Along with many hours spent working on my books and keeping in touch with my readers.

A big thank you to my extended family who support me being a book enthusiast.

A huge thank you to my editor, Neila F., her editing and writing tips, and my Proofreader, Libybet R. G., for picking up the things we missed.

Thank you to all of my readers who have loved my work, and continue to read my stories. I would love for you to share your thoughts in a review on one or all of the following:

Amazon.com
Goodreads
Barnes & Noble
You can follow Katrina Cope at:

https://www.facebook.com/Author.Katrina.Cope

https://twitter.com/Katrina_R_Cope

https://www.goodreads.com/author/show/7265107.Katrina_Cope

https://www.katrinacopebooks.com

http://http://www.amazon.com/Katrina-Cope/e/B00F00JF9M/

BOOKS BY KATRINA COPE

~~~~~

Pre-Teen Books

THE SANCTUM SERIES

JAYDEN'S CYBERMOUNTAIN

SCARLET'S ESCAPE

TAYLOR'S PLIGHT

ERIC & THE BLACK AXES

ADRIANNA'S SURGE

~~~~~

Young Adult Urban Fantasy

AFTERLIFE SERIES

FLEDGLING

THE TAKING

ANGELIC RETRIBUTION

DIVIDED PATHS

Afterlife Novelette

THE GATEKEEPER

~~~~~

Young Adult Urban Paranormal Fantasy

SUPERNATURAL EVOLVEMENT SERIES

(Associated with the Afterlife Series)

WITCH'S LEGACY (#0.5 Prequel)

AALIYAH

~~~~~

Young Adult Fantasy Nordic Myths

VALKYRIE ACADEMY DRAGON ALLIANCE

SERIES

MARKED (Prequel)

CHOSEN

VANISHED

SCORNED

INFLICTED

EMPOWERED

AMBUSHED

WARNED

ABDUCTED

BESIEGED

DECEIVED

DID YOU ENJOY THIS BOOK?
YOU CAN MAKE A BIG DIFFERENCE.

Honest reviews of my books help bring them to the attention of other readers.

If you've enjoyed this book, I'd be grateful if you could spend a few minutes leaving a review (it can be as short as you like).
The review can be left on Amazon and Goodreads.
Thank you very much.

ABOUT THE AUTHOR

Katrina is an author of several Young Adult and Preteen/Middle Grade novels. Each of her released books reaching the top 100 in certain categories on the Amazon's Best Sellers Rank – a few even as high as number one.

She resides in Queensland, Australia. Her three teenage boys and husband for over nineteen years treat her like a princess. Unfortunately though, this princess still has to do domestic chores.

From a very young age, she has been a very creative person and has spent many years travelling the world and observing many different personalities and cultures. Her favourite personalities have been the strange ones, yet the ones under the radar also hold a place in her heart.

During her last extensive travels, she spent 16 nights in a bomb shelter on a Kibbutz 8 kilometers off the Lebanese border. It was to avoid Katyusha bombs that the resident volunteers decided to name her after (she is still trying to work out why).

Katrina's online home is at
www.katrinacopebooks.com

You can connect with Katrina on:
Twitter https://twitter.com/Katrina_R_Cope
Facebook
https://www.facebook.com/Author.Katrina.Cope
Instagram
https://www.instagram.com/katrina_cope_author
Pinterest
https://www.pinterest.com.au/katrinacope56
Email authorkatrinacope@gmail.com